Affliction

A Collection of Short Stories About Bullies

Written by
James Penn

Illustrations
Tyler Stachowicz
Jeff Skidmore
James Penn

Book Layout & Design
James Penn

Affliction
A Collection of Short Stories About Bullies

Illustrations appear as follows:
Dedication Page, Kerosene: Tyler Stachowicz
Affliction: James Penn
Troll, PTSD, Superhero: Jeff Skidmore

ISBN-13: 978-0-615-93045-9
ISBN-10: 061593045X

This book was typeset in Adobe Garamond Pro and Marker Felt

Printed in the United States of America

CreateSpace
7290 Investment Drive Suite B
North Charleston, SC 29418
866.362.8262
(tws.createspace.com)

This book is dedicated to everyone who is or has ever been a victim of bullying. Stay strong and don't let them destroy your spirit.

Table of Contents

Preface

Affliction was written to focus the reader's attention on the issue of modern-day bullying. During my research, I found a multitude of toll-free helplines and informative self-help guides offering guidance on how to handle being bullied, but very few writers have allowed this topic to serve as the foundation of a fictitious work.

Bullying has exceeded the trivialities of stealing a child's lunch money and its ramifications are far more complex than a blackened eye. Social withdrawal, sleep disorders, depression, declining grades, aggressive behavior and suicide are just a few of the appalling realities of victimization.

Hearing and reading factual accounts of children and teens who have experienced persecution from their peers inspired me to write this book. Composing five stories that not only describe the physical and emotional aspects of bullying, but also exposes the ways bullies target, was my goal.

Placing the characters in realistic situations, creating depth and interweaving explicit language, give these stories an authentic, gripping edge. The hook to these narratives is the protagonist's rise above victimization. These stories could have been written as dark tragedies that resulted in the victim's untimely demise, but I gave my heroes a strong persona where, even on the threshold of psychological collapse, they discover their inner-strength and refuse to be defeated by recognizing their own self-worth.

If you happen to be one of the countless victims suffering as a result of these relentless acts of punishment, remember, you have a choice and there is always a way out. It isn't achieved through violence or self-destruction, but through personal acceptance, staying true to yourself and, above all, staying strong.

James Penn

Kerosene

Dylan had stepped onto his muddy length of driveway when a car came to a screeching halt behind him. The ominous vehicle rumbled and sputtered as it sat idling on the blacktop. Jake revved the super-charged engine to boast, and a bloodcurdling growl from underneath the hood rattled Dylan's nerves and twisted his guts into an overwrought bundle of knots.

"QUEER!" Jake hollered.

Matt launched his can of soda from the passenger side window. It zoomed through the air like a rocket before exploding against the small of Dylan's back. Uncontrollable laughter spilled out of the car and echoed through the surrounding of amber-colored hollows.

"Assholes," Dylan hissed, sucking the pain through his teeth.

Everyday was the same and Dylan hated it. He

hated high school. He hated his life. He hated Jake and Matt even more. He especially hated being picked on and called names like queer, punk, homo and freak, because they were false assumptions fabricated by two narrow-minded boys.

Jake thrust the tricked-out deathtrap in reverse and backed into an overgrown lot beside the road where a weathered sign, hanging from a piece of rope, gave its warning to trespassers.

"I'm gonna kick your ass!" Jake yelled as he and Matt charged across the pavement.

Dylan bolted down the path to make his escape, but Jake, who prided himself on his athletic agility, opted on a shorter route through the woods to head him off.

The untied shoelace in his trashed pair of Converse and the backpack weighing on his shoulder prevented Dylan from making the get-away he had hoped for. His reddened cheeks were raw and tingly from running in the crisp autumn wind. Matt was close on his heels and shouted crude, vile obscenities. A few yards ahead, Jake stood tall and confident, arms folded and wearing a smug look. Once again, Dylan found himself trapped.

"Didn't think an ass-pirate like you could run so fast," Matt teased, "Coach Adkins could use you on the team."

"No, dude, shaking pompoms is more his speed," said Jake, staring down his prey.

"Rah! Rah! Rah!" Matt cheered.

Underneath Dylan's shroud of fear, laid the resentment he felt for the two. "Idiots," he muttered, and tried to force his way through them.

"What did you say, homo?" Jake asked as he pushed Dylan backward with a forceful hand.

"The little shit-head called us idiots," Matt repeated.

Jake frowned and got up real close in Dylan's face; his massive ego and threatening demeanor was simply a coward's cloak.

"I'll stomp your ass right here and now."

Dylan wanted to give Jake a mouthful, but he played it safe and kept silent.

"He probably enjoys getting his ass stomped," Matt surmised.

Jake gave Dylan a once over, sizing him up and said, "Enjoys it? He probably gets off on it."

"That's freakin' sick, bro," Matt said, but laughed just the same.

Dylan held white-knuckled fists down at his sides. He wanted to play a tough guy and nail Jake good, but knew the outcome could be grim. Deadly.

"That is kinda gross," Jake agreed, "but I bet that soda can hurt like a bitch, though."

"Yeah," Matt replied, "let's have a looksee."

Dylan backed away in protest. Jake intercepted and held him with an iron grip while Matt yanked the backpack from his shoulder and raised the shirt halfway up his back. An irritated, puffy spot had formed above the waist of his skinny jeans.

"Nice!" Matt said proudly, critiquing his work. "And I wasn't even trying hard."

"It's gonna bruise up good, too." Jake added.

Dylan felt violated by the odd procedure. Jake released him after he and Matt had completed their examination.

"Can I have my backpack, now?" Dylan asked.

Matt dangled it in the air by one strap. "You mean this backpack?" He asked, being facetious.

"C'mon. Just give it to me. Alright?"

"If you want it, come get it."

Dylan lunged for it. Matt tossed it to Jake. Their petty game ended when the over-stuffed bag found its way into a large puddle of mud. As Dylan rushed to save his drowning satchel, Jake used every muscle in his arm to deliver a whopper punch that hit dead center of the soda can wound. The unexpected blow brought Dylan to his knees and near the brink of tears.

"I'll deal with you later," he promised, and then turned to his accomplice. "Let's go. I don't have time to play with this retard all afternoon."

The rowdy boys howled like wolves relishing the moment of their cowardly deed. Squalling tires left streaks of burnt rubber on the asphalt. Dylan prayed for the vehicle to flip and crash as Jake challenged Daredevil's Curve.

After finding the front door locked, Dylan ventured to his bedroom window and pried the screen loose. He slid the glass pane up, threw his backpack inside and sprang upward to hoist himself. Scrawny legs wrapped in tight denim kicked at the air as he swam through. Magazine cutouts of his favorite rock bands and pages of disturbing literature by Edgar Allan Poe adorned the walls.

He peeled off the soda-drenched shirt, exposing his protruding rib bones and sunken tummy, then stood in front of the mirror to examine the newest addition to his collection of scars. Shades of yellow and purple outlined the swollen area. Previous encounters with Matt and Jake were tattooed in his flesh and even deeper in his mind. Turning away from the loser staring back at him, Dylan grabbed a black T-shirt from the heap of dirty clothes piled on the floor.

Dylan fantasized often of ways to escape his tormentors. He relaxed against the wall, in the corner, closed his eyes and created a plan to rid himself of the menacing pair. In his scenario, he swipes the unopened bottle of whiskey his mom hid behind the pots and pans under the kitchen counter. After the football game is the perfect opportunity to lure them into his trap. Excitement fills their eyes when he opens his backpack to show them the full bottle. Oh, how simple it would be! They'll never suspect a thing. The abandoned church is an ideal spot to drink without being seen. There, his surprise will be waiting. Once inside, the three of them drink, goof-off and talk guy stuff: football games, fast cars and scoring with hot girls from school. Jake and Matt declare him "The coolest friend ever" and they toast "To friendship!" Midnight has crept upon them as well as drunkenness and Dylan is boiling over with anticipation waiting for them to pass out. Oh, yes! The moment has arrived! He positions their limp bodies against the dank stones and gets to work. Those rusty chains dad uses to hitch things to the truck come in handy. Reviving from a drunken stupor, the intoxicated boys find themselves bound to the wall and Dylan laying brick before their eyes. They yell for help, but what's the use? No one will hear their cries that deep in the woods.

"Okay, you little prick, you've played your joke. Now unchain us!" Jake demands.

Dylan pays no mind; the chalky smell of mortar has him in a psychotic trance.

"Hey, dick head!" Matt yells. "You better let us go, or you'll be sorry!"

Beneath their hard-shelled exterior lies their fear, which is rising as fast as the wall before them. Dylan hears the rhythmic thump of his own heart and finds the sensation of being in control morbidly stimulating. But his scheme is not yet complete. Just before he sets the last brick into place, he tosses a can of soda inside.

"In case you get thirsty," he says, and finishes sealing them in, savoring the moment of his revenge.

It would be another late night for Dylan's mother. Left to his own devices, he rummaged through the kitchen in search of something to silence his groaning stomach. Ham and withered lettuce between slices of stale bread would have to suffice. Afterward, he stretched out on the bedroom floor to complete his homework.

As night approached, it grew unseasonably cold and, like an uninvited guest, the chill forced its way inside. Dylan grabbed a book of matches to light the heater, but the fuel gauge read empty. He journeyed to the back porch for the kerosene jug only to discover that it, too, was bone dry. Feeling discouraged, he set out for the gas station with the empty container and a few dollars he took from his parent's money jar.

Outside, blustery winds swayed majestic pines and whistled through bending trees. Frosty air sliced through Dylan's T-shirt. His hand searched for warmth in his jeans pocket. To distract himself from the cold, he imagined living in a better environment where the house was clean and his parents would inquire about his day rather than bash him all the time. In his fantasy, a hot meal would be on the dinner table every night. He marveled at the convenience of adjusting the thermostat when it grew nippy, instead of walking to buy fuel. How comforting it must be to have parents who are loving and responsible.

The gas station was miles away and, being Friday night, traffic from the high school football game would crowd the streets soon. Dylan wasted no time at the pump and rushed home to avoid being seen with the embarrassing red container. He had passed the spooky trail leading to the abandoned church and crossed the one lane bridge, when a car recklessly approached from behind. Tires screeched as it swerved to the opposite side of the road forcing Dylan to the shoulder.

"Get out of the way, freak!" Jake screamed as he blew past.

"Jerk-offs," Dylan said.

The road grew darker and scarier the closer he got toward home, especially around Daredevil's Curve, where a canopy of oak tree branches prevented any gleam of moonlight from shining through.

"It's not smart to walk alone out here," Jake said with a sinister grin, "you never know what kind of trouble you'll run into."

Dylan froze. His stomach knotted up again. He felt sick and started to sweat a little. Jake was leaned against the front fender, grinding his fist into his palm. His scheme to park in a well-hidden area near Daredevil's Curve and wait for Dylan to blunder by had worked like a charm.

"You're gonna get it this time," Matt promised.

Dylan clutched the handle of the kerosene jug, and without giving it a second thought, he fled into the woods like a scared rabbit.

"Go ahead and run, pussy! I'll hunt you down even if it takes all night!" Jake hollered, racing in after him.

Boney twigs and razor-sharp thorns clawed at Dylan's naked arms, holding him back. His heart pounded in his chest. A baseball-size lump of fright hung in his throat as he pushed himself through the lightless, timbered confusion. Being forced to go hunting with his dad had taught him how to move swiftly and silently and camouflage himself. He would have gotten away if he hadn't lost his footing on a gathering of slick leaves. The plastic container flew out of his hand and disappeared into the darkness. Jake caught up just in time to break his fall. He grabbed a handful of T-shirt, dragged Dylan to the car and shoved him inside.

"You're dead meat," he said, eyeing Dylan through the rearview and floored it with disregard for the 35 mile per hour speed limit.

The inside of Jake's car smelled nauseously familiar; he and Matt were sharing a bottle of whiskey, but it wasn't the cheap stuff Dylan's mom drank. Jake turned up the bottle and chugged. His cell phone started buzzing with text messages from his girlfriend Skyler, who demanded the 4-1-1 on his whereabouts. Jake didn't bother texting back, as the problem in his backseat required his immediate attention.

He turned onto a narrow trail with overgrown weeds bordering its sides. The bumpy, winding path seemed endless. Just ahead were the skeletal remains of the neglected, stone church Dylan fantasized about sealing Matt and Jake inside of. The frightful, old structure gleamed under the pale moonlight. Ominous shadows lurking behind condemned walls watched through vandalized windows and greeted them with an unnerving welcome.

Dylan's stomach sank into the floorboard when the car stopped. After getting snatched from the backseat, he stood in the cold with his arms folded to keep from freezing. He was terrified and his teeth were busily chattering. Matt stood beside the car guzzling booze.

"Dude, chill!" Jake barked. "You think it was easy swiping that from my dad's liquor cabinet? Give it here."

Matt took a hefty gulp before passing it over. Jake, in turn, took a few heaping swigs, then reached way down for a thunderous belch. He handed-off the bottle, frowned at Dylan and said, "I told you I was gonna deal with you later."

Without thinking, Dylan fired off, "Well, do it and get it over with, you arrogant dick!"

Jake had had a bellyful of Dylan's name-calling even though he was guilty of the same offense. But being the aggressor, he felt entitled, and receiving anything less than the respect he demanded, was an insult to his rank. He lost all sense of control and threw one heck of a punch. A fistful of head-splitting pain passed through Dylan's skull.

"You wanna act tough and talk shit?" Jake delivered a second punch. "Let's see if you can back it up."

The third blow caught Dylan's eye and laid him on the ground. His throbbing face found relief in the cold leaves. Matt finished off the booze and tossed the bottle.

"Yeah, bro! Kick his ass!" he said.

Before Dylan could get on his feet, Jake knocked him down again and started kicking him in the ribs.

"You got something else you wanna say?" Jake asked, booting Dylan's sides. "Do you, asshole?"

Dylan curled his body and shielded his torso from the jolt of every agonizing kick.

"Go to hell," he wheezed.

Jake pulled Dylan to his feet and leaned him against the trunk. Ripples of pain tore through his body while Jake clobbered his face and abdomen. Dylan wanted to vomit his guts, but his dinner spilled out instead.

"You little shit!" Jake said, looking down at the disgusting bits of regurgitated ham, lettuce and bread that had spewed all over his brand new sneakers.

After receiving another punch, Dylan fell to the earth with barely enough strength to crawl away. Jake squashed his back like a bug, flipped him over and straddled him. The bulk of muscular mass pressing into Dylan's midsection felt like a hundred red-hot pokers stabbing his guts. He struggled to throw Jake off of him, but was too puny and weak. He felt around for a rock, a stick, anything substantial that he could use to defend himself; he found the whiskey bottle.

Knowing there was no other option for survival, Dylan gripped the neck, firmly, and whacked him over the head. The bottle shattered into pieces. His underhanded maneuver caught Jake off guard and allowed him to prepare for another strike. The makeshift weapon glistened as he brought it down. Jagged edges ripped Jake's left cheek.

"MOTHERFUCKER!" he roared, and slammed Dylan's wrist on the ground to release the sharp fragment from his grasp. "STUPID QUEER!"

Jake went out of his mind and continued to beat him senseless.

"Get off him," Matt said nervously, realizing Jake had carried his game too far.

But Jake wouldn't stop; the rip in his face fueled his anger. He raised Dylan's head to throw a final punch. It hit the ground with a thud. Blood spattered out of his mouth as he choked.

"Dude, let's go," Matt said, practically forcing Jake into the car.

Jake grabbed his gym towel from the backseat to soak up the blood pouring down his shredded face.

"You better watch your back, 'cause next time, you're freakin' dead!" Jake warned, and sped off.

Dylan regained consciousness an hour later chilled to the core, with a few cracked ribs, a busted lip, a swollen eye and found the abandoned sanctuary laughing at the irony. Not even the ruins of a holy place felt welcoming.

He limped out of the woods and concentrated on getting home. His thoughts quickly shifted to Jake and Matt. He wanted to get even. But what could he do? Tell his parents? Whatever. Talk to his teachers? Too cliché. Go to the police? What a joke. No, tattle telling was petty and weak. They needed to suffer.

Luckily, the wind had died down some, but the road remained dark and deserted. After Dylan crossed the one lane bridge, he began reliving the nightmarish events of the evening. He remembered losing the kerosene jug somewhere close by and began searching for it. While he hunted, a muffled tune carried over the wind. He followed the noise a couple of feet or so and as he got closer, an eerie light gleamed under a scattering of leaves. Dylan gently kicked the foliage off with his foot, uncovering a cell phone that had somehow found its way into the woods. The screen was a spider web of cracks and there was no way to identify the caller. After deciding not to answer it, he put it to good use by letting it serve as a makeshift flashlight. On its side, not far from where he fell, lay the jug.

"If dad had of filled up before going out on the road, none of this would've happened," he griped.

Daredevil's Curve was painted with fresh tire marks and the bloody, mutilated carcass of a full-grown deer lay next to them. Its neck was twisted backward. Huge, black, glassy eyes stared into oblivion. The hind legs kicked as it struggled to breathe. Dylan felt sorry for the creature and wanted to put it out of its misery, although he never had the courage to end his own.

He stayed with it until all the life had drained onto the street. Experiencing death up close inspired Dylan to plot his own demise. What about a bullet through the head or plunging off the one lane bridge? A noose around the neck would probably do the trick. His thoughts of a better existence were interrupted by faint cries of help in the darkness. He pursued the wailing to a brushy area that had recently been plowed through and walked about a hundred paces before stumbling upon a car wedged between two trees. Impact from the collision had rammed the driver's seat forward, pinning the driver between it and the steering wheel.

The light from the cell phone went dim. Dylan brushed his thumb across the screen to illuminate it and held it up to the busted-out window. Jake was banged up good with deep cuts and abrasions. His pupils were large and strained from too much booze. His left eye, which had been torn by a shard of glass, was a grotesque bloody sphere. Matt was slumped over and unconscious, but shared similar injuries.

"Who's that?" Jake asked, squinting the light out of his eyes.

"That deer you hit died," Dylan answered, his tone sad, almost apologetic.

Blood leaked from the gash in Jake's forehead and trickled down his nose. "What?" he asked confused and stunned over it all.

"It was just lying there hurt and alone."

"I hit a deer?"

Jake's unwise decision to text while driving, not to mention his alcohol intake, is what prevented him from seeing the deer in the first place.

"There's blood everywhere—and its neck," Dylan paused. "But it's dead now, so..."

"Screw that deer! We need help!" Jake snapped.

The cell phone rang again. His eyes shot wide open when he heard the familiar ringtone.

"Dude, that's my phone!" he exclaimed. "Skyler's calling. Answer it and tell her I've been in an accident!"

For some unforeseen reason while having a brief moment of remorse, Dylan considered helping them.

Maybe they would be grateful and the bullying would stop? He thought.

Matt groaned as he came to. Dylan readied his thumb to receive the call. He knew telling Skyler about the accident and getting them help was the humane thing to do, then doubt set in. He stared blankly at the screen debating whether or not to answer it. By the time he had rationalized the situation and was about to answer it, Jake had grown impatient.

"Answer the phone you stupid dick wad!"

The vile things Jake spat out of his mouth quickly brought Dylan to his senses and he retraced his steps to the road.

"Where are you going? Come back here!"

Dylan's kerosene jug was sitting on the road, beside the deer, where he left it. Completely fed up with the pair of them, he seized the opportunity lying before him and returned to the banged-up car. Jake was muttering blasphemous things under his breath and Matt, who was now fully awake, was covered in his own vomit.

Skyler had the phone in a tizzy between her onslaught of text messages and back-to-back calling. Dylan shoved the annoying device in his pocket, unscrewed the spout and began pouring kerosene on the smashed hood.

"What the hell are you doing?" Jake asked.

"You little shit!" Matt hollered. "This ain't funny! Stop messing around!"

Dylan tossed some of the rancid fluid through Jake's busted-out window and quietly worked his way around the car. Matt was freaking out and rammed his shoulder against the barricaded door trying to open it.

"It's all Jake's fault!" he blabbed, trying to save his own skin. "You'd be dead right now if I hadn't pulled him off you."

Matt's betrayal cut Jake deeper than the whiskey bottle. Their tight-knit bond slowly began to unravel.

"Stop whining like a little bitch. And don't try to pin all this on me. It was your idea to take him to the abandoned church grounds!"

"Yeah, to mess with him some. I didn't know you were gonna beat him half to death!"

Out of all the times Dylan fantasized about luring Jake and Matt onto the abandoned church grounds, not once did it cross his mind that they were plotting too. After hearing Matt's confession, he poured on even more fluid. By the time he finished his task, there was barely enough fuel left for the heater at home.

"This shit is whack!" Jake screeched. "When I get out of this, I swear to God I'm gonna kill your punk ass!"

Dylan sat the container on the ground and pulled the matches out of his pocket. He stared at them with a blank look and said, "Do you have any idea what it's like to be pushed around, beaten up and treated like shit, just because someone else thinks its cool? Have you ever thought about killing yourself because, somehow, being dead would be better than getting pounded everyday? Do you have any idea what it's like to feel nothing but emptiness and pain?"

He flipped the paper cover back then plucked a match from the first row.

"You think you're tough because you can kick my ass and make my life shit. In reality, you're just a couple of losers who get a hard-on from beating up on guys who can't defend themselves."

"Screw you, asshole!" Matt yelled, still pushing against the door. "You wouldn't be sayin' that if we weren't trapped in here!"

Jake tried grabbing the lever under the seat, to unjam it, but failed. Excruciating pain in his dislocated shoulder made him curse.

"Mother—!" he bellowed. "You're one dead fag, you hear me?" An undertone of panic lay in his words.

Getting even wasn't quite what Dylan had anticipated. It was more exhilarating when he fantasized about it. In real life, there was no rush of adrenaline, no orgasmic high, no gratifying feeling of justice. In a way, he felt cheated.

The match popped as it scratched the grainy strip, and a tiny spark danced into a bright orange flame. It was there, inside the warm glow, where Dylan saw his peace, his solace and his salvation. He yearned to light them up and blast them straight to hell.

"With all the shit I've taken from you," he began, "it wouldn't phase me to set this car on fire. Believe me, I would enjoy watching both of you burn."

Jake and Matt fearfully awaited Dylan's next move. Neither one of them were ready to die such an unimaginable death. They looked as though they had pissed their pants, or worse. And although he wanted to, Dylan's conscience wouldn't allow it. He let the match fall from the pinch of his numb fingertips and collected the kerosene jug.

Before heading home and leaving them totally abandoned, he reached in his pocket for Jake's shattered phone.

"I could've set you on fire and not thought twice about it," he said, and tossed it through the busted out window, "but I didn't, because that's not who I am—I'm better than that."

Affliction

"I HATE THEM!" Cole shouted. Tears of rage and anguish streamed down his bruised face.

He punched his pillow, then the wall. He even pounded his head to rid his mind of the assault that took place five minutes ago.

It didn't work.

Yellow dots flickered in front of his eyes when he opened them. His temples throbbed. His head ached. He breathed deep to defuse his anger. Although the pent-up rage was gone, the anguish remained.

Cole fell onto the bed and stared gloomily at the bracelet of handprints circling his wrists. That's where Brad, better known as "Mouth", held his arms behind his back so Stu could get in a good punch. He could still feel the tightness of Mouth's fat hands crushing them. They were tender and throbbed with pain, and those handprints were going to be plum-colored by

33

morning. It made him nauseous knowing the kids at school would see them and perceive him as a weakling who couldn't stand up to Mouth and Stu.

"I should get dad's straight razor and have at it," he said to himself, "who would even care or even miss me?"

He could rule out Mouth and Stu, and his dad wouldn't either. He doesn't seem to care about anything anymore. After Cole's mom died, his dad went off the deep-end and started boozing it up, drowning his sorrows, ignoring his responsibilities and becoming more violent each day. Then Cole grew to hate him. Sometimes, he wished his dad would go away and never come back. He hates it when he comes home from work intoxicated, beats and yells at him for no reason and then covers his guilt by drinking until he passes out on the couch or the floor.

"I miss mom," he sobbed.

His eyes flooded again and the bedroom went all blurry. He snatched her picture off of his nightstand and said, "Why did you have to die and leave me here to deal with this by myself?"

He fell asleep shortly after reading the inspirational words she dedicated to him on the back of it. He often read the inscription so he could feel close to her, feel safe and feel loved. Nothing or no one in the backwoods town of Chipper Creek lived up to its name.

Excessive noise, outbursts of profanity and cabinet doors slamming in the kitchen abruptly woke Cole out of his sleep.

Dad was home.

Glowing numbers on the alarm clock, beside Cole's bed, flashed 10:58. He didn't realize he had slept for almost seven hours. He lay there and listened hard at the muffled voices coming from the living room and realized it was only the TV.

"Wherths sit at?" his dad slurred to himself. He was drunk. Again.

"I know I put tha damn thing in here!"

Heavy footsteps shuffled down the hallway. Cole shut his eyes tight and pretended to be asleep. A loud thud hit the frame of his bedroom door.

"Son-of-a-bitch!" his dad swore.

He propped his weight against the doorjamb of Cole's bedroom. The walls were closing in and the floor was spinning. He stood in the doorway trying to get a grip on his reality. Cole cringed and prayed for a quick beating.

"Wherths sit at, boy?" his dad demanded. "I know you got it!"

Cole lay perfectly still and didn't make a sound.

"What did I tell you about messin' with my stuff?"

Cole wished he did have that bottle opener his dad was looking for; it would be one less beer swimming through his system.

He was sweating under the sheets and felt a prickly, numbing sensation in his toes. The feeling slowly progressed to the top of his head. It wasn't the sort of tingle one gets when you're excited or know something wonderful is about to happen. It was a dreaded fearful feeling because he knew that he was about to get it. Big-time.

"Mus' be asleep," his dad said, and staggered toward his own bedroom and slammed the door.

Cole woke the next morning at seven, still dressed in his clothes from the day before. He didn't want to get up. He didn't want to go to school and just "deal" with it. He didn't want another confrontation with Mouth and Stu, either.

Cole stared at the wall beside his bed until his eyes began to water then pushed his covers down to examine his wrists. They weren't going to be much use to him for the next day or two.

It was twenty minutes til eight and Cole's dad wasn't up. He had already been written-up twice for being late and missing too many days. If he wasn't at work on time Johnny, the lead mechanic at E-Z Greasy Garage, was going to fire him. Cole reluctantly stepped into the bedroom to wake him.

"Dad," he called in a whisper.

He was sleeping hard and snoring loudly. Milky saliva oozed from the corner of his mouth and onto the pillow. He reeked of old cigarette butts and beer. Cole tried again, this time using a forceful nudge.

"You're gonna be late."

He shifted his body, grunted and mumbled vulgarities into the drool-encrusted pillow.

"DAD! WAKE UP!"

Suddenly Cole felt a sharp, white-hot pain in his gut and fell back against the wall. It happened so quick, it took a moment for him to realize he had been elbowed.

"I'll get up when I'm good and damn ready," his dad snarled.

Cole sat pain-stricken on the bedroom floor wanting to cry, wanting to curse—wanting to bash his dad's skull in with the baseball bat he kept under his bed.

"You should get ready for work," he said, and stood up. "You don't need to get written-up again."

"Don't worry about what I need! Just make sure that wood gets stacked up in the shed before I get home! Hear me, boy?"

Cole was infuriated and didn't respond. He stormed out to catch the bus for school.

Dense fog had drifted in and settled upon the rolling hills of Chipper Creek. It was gray and damp outside, and the absence of life suggested a bleak, depressing mood. The apple orchards Cole and his mom used to frequent on summer evenings, once picturesque with country charm, had been left gnarled and barren by the change of season.

Ghastly details of yesterday's ambush replayed vividly in his mind as Cole approached the place where it happened.

"Where you goin' ass-wipe?" Mouth asked. He was all puffed up and his sweatshirt was stretched to the max across his broad shoulders and protruding belly.

He and Stu moved in close, trapping him.

"Move!" Cole demanded.

"Who's gonna make us?" Stu chuckled. "*You?*" His ball cap was strategically cocked to one side. The effect added to his relaxed and negligent appearance.

"He's too much of a punk ass mama's boy to make us do anything," Mouth said, and shoved him. "Do you need your mommy to save you?" He taunted.

Cole felt his anger welling up inside. Name-calling and shoving was one thing, but using his dead mother in their bully tactic crossed a boundary and treaded upon a well-guarded, sacred territory.

Stu looked hard into Cole's eyes. "Get over it, mama's boy," he said. "She can't save you—she's six feet deep in maggots!"

The callous remark tossed kindling on the fire that lay smoldering within the pit of Cole's soul.

"SHUT YOUR DAMN MOUTH!" he yelled, and pushed Stu against the wooden fence that bordered the orchards. "DON'T EVER SAY THAT!"

"Get this punk off me!" Stu yelled.

That's when Mouth grabbed his wrists and pulled his arms behind his back. The more Cole resisted, the tighter Mouth squeezed to restrain him.

"Listen, dick splash, nobody tells *me* to shut up!" Stu said as he pushed up the sleeves of his hoodie. "Now you're gonna pay," he promised, and began pounding Cole's face with a fat round fist.

The bus threw on its caution lights as it approached Cole's stop and opened its doors. He collected his nerves and trudged up the steps dreading whatever lay in store for him at school.

It was the longest day ever, time creeping at a snail's pace. Cole had only been at school for a couple of hours, but it seemed like forever. All day long he stared at the clock and wished he could make the rest of the day fly by or better yet, make himself disappear.

The three o'clock bell rang. He jumped out of his seat and hurried to the restroom to beat the crowd. He stood at the urinal and watched nervously over his shoulder, willing the continuous stream of golden fluid to stop. Then he quickly buttoned his fly so he wouldn't miss the bus.

"Well, well," Stu said, crossing his arms. "Looks like you're in the wrong restroom, mama's boy."

"Yeah," Mouth agreed. "How did you manage that standing up? I thought girls squatted when they took a piss?"

Cole was tired of their crap and imagined ramming Mouth's fat head into the hard, white porcelain. He turned around, fists clinched and ready. He knew he couldn't take them, but he wanted to at least try to defend himself.

"Leave me alone or else!" he warned, holding two fistfuls of confidence in front of his chest.

Mouth and Stu chuckled at his tough act.

"Or else what, you big sissy? You gonna tell on us?" Mouth asked, and shoved him against the cold, grimy wall.

Cole's eyes darted from one boy to the other. He knew not to say another word. He wished he had of gone straight to the bus instead of stopping by the restroom. He wished he had of held it until he got home.

Stu stepped closer and said, "You got a death wish or something, standing there and threatening us?"

Cole swallowed hard. The courage he possessed a moment ago had dwindled down to zero.

"I wouldn't be shootin' my mouth off to anybody if I were you." Stu cracked his knuckles. "It's time I taught you a lesson."

Mouth knew that was code for him to go to the door and keep a lookout.

"Please don't hurt me," Cole begged.

"Hurt you?" Stu sneered, "I'm gonna choke the worthless life right outta you."

The last time Cole had hands wrapped around his throat was two months ago, when his dad came home and found the contents of his twelve-pack poured down the kitchen sink.

Cole's face turned beet-red and then bluish-purple as Stu crushed his windpipe to smithereens with one hand. He wrestled with Stu's forearm and even tried prying his fingers away, but Stu wasn't letting go. The look in his eyes grew crazed and wild, and his smile revealed the pleasure he derived from Cole's fear. Cole became lightheaded and the restroom began to fade, as Stu's grip kept getting tighter.

"Teacher's coming!" Mouth warned.

Stu's delight turned to disappointment when he released Cole.

"You're lucky," he said.

Cole collapsed to the floor, gagging. A thin string of spit dribbled out of his mouth.

"He's such a little bitch," Mouth said, shaking his head.

"Hope you have an awesome weekend," Stu said, and took a quick glance at himself in the mirror, "because Monday's the start of a whole new week."

Cole was half a second shy of missing the bus. Feeling self-conscious over the marks on his neck, he dropped his head as he passed the rows of seats so none of the other kids would see them. He slumped down in an empty seat at the back, wiped a clear streak through the build up of condensation on the window and looked out at the passing trees and houses.

The fog was a heavy, gray mass and a mist of rain began to spray just as Cole stepped off the bus. He was annoyed for backing down from Stu in the restroom when he should've been fighting back.

"They know I'm a wimp for sure," he said to himself.

The reality made him feel worse. There was no telling how far Mouth and Stu would go to make his life miserable. The marks on his neck were proof of that. Cole felt like an outsider and there was no one he could turn to or trust. Getting the support he needed from his dad was out of the question and reporting them to school administration would only add to his problems.

Instead of going straight home to do his chores, Cole wandered into the orchard and sat under his favorite tree, the one he and his mom used to sit under and talk. The ground was wet and soggy, but he didn't care, this was the only place he felt happy, protected and sane. No one could bother him here.

"Out of all the trees in this orchard," his mom would begin, "this one grows the sweetest and juiciest apples, because it's flawed and not as perfect as the rest. So it proves its worth in a different way."

It always used to make him smile when she would say that. Finding the good in things was one of her many charismatic traits. That's how she coped with the cancer that took her away from him six months ago. He wished she were here now to make him smile and tell him that everything was going to be ok. Then he remembered Her birthday is tomorrow. He'd make it priority to visit her grave in the morning.

Large, cold drops of rain fell from an ashen sky, awakening Cole from his unintended nap.

"Shit!" he exclaimed, as he scrambled to his feet.

He ran home mortified over the unimaginable things his dad would do to him for not having the wood stacked in the shed. He realized how foolish he was to be rushing to his doom rather than taking his time and sparing himself the grief.

Maybe he hasn't been home long enough to get wasted and he'll be sober and cool about the whole thing? Maybe he's had one-too-many and is passed out on the couch? Maybe he's not home yet and I still have time to get the wood stacked before he gets there? Maybe if I explain, he'll understand?

Cole's hopeful ideas were quickly shot down when he saw his dad's big silver truck parked in the yard.

He would prefer to have stayed the night under the apple tree in the pouring rain rather than face the monster inside. He thought it wise to avoid the confrontation by getting his chore done before going into the house, that way his dad couldn't do anything to him. Much.

"Where the hell have you been?" a gruff voice asked from a dark corner of the shed.

Cole had been caught off-guard and red-handed. He quaked with apprehension. He was convinced that his dad planned it this way, just so he could have a reason to knock him around.

"I thought I said to have this wood stacked before I got home."

His voice was heavier and coarser than normal, like he had just got up. Cole parted his lips to explain, but nothing came out. His throat was sore and dry. He stood in the threshold of the shed with torrents of rain falling behind him.

"Sorry, Dad," he managed and frantically piled wood in his arms.

By the time he had collected a weighty stack, his dad had walked over and stood behind him. Cole, unaware of his presence, was startled when he turned around. The wood fell out of his arms and rolled onto the ground. His heart leaped into his throat as he stared nervously into his dad's bloodshot eyes and braced himself for a backhand.

"It's about time you got home," his dad said, and walked into the house.

Cole couldn't believe it; he thought for sure he was going to get the beating of a lifetime. He had gotten all bent out of shape and prepared himself for the worse, and for what? He went back to his chore confused over it all.

Why was dad waiting in the shed for me all that time, just to say what he did, and not punish me for not having the wood stacked up? Something's not right. Why was I in such a hurry to get home to receive a beating in the first place? Who does that? Am I really that messed up that I feel like I'm not entitled to a normal, abuse-free life? That's retarded! Have I gotten so used to being bullied by Dad, Mouth and Stu, that I feel let down when it doesn't happen? I must be insane! Why do I feel worse now than I did when I was being choked in the restroom? And how do I get over this disorder that keeps me in torment?

Last night was like a weird dream; Cole was still perplexed over his dad's less-than-normal behavior. He got dressed in a hurry and raced to the cemetery.

Cutting through the woods and entering the graveyard from the rear was faster than walking across town. He had passed the first few rows of granite markers when he spotted a silver truck parked near the entrance of the five-acre cemetery. Cole dashed behind an ornate monument and watched. His dad was stooped on one knee and his left hand rested on top of his wife's headstone. After holding that position for several minutes, he stood up, wiped his eyes with the cuff of his thermal jacket and dropped a small bouquet of flowers on the grave. Cole waited until he was in the truck and out of sight before investigating.

He picked up the arrangement of tiger lilies, snapdragons, and daisies, her favorites, and propped them up neatly against the headstone. A small notecard with "Chickpea" written across the envelope fell out of the flowers. Chickpea was his dad's nickname for her when he was in an exceptionally pleasant mood or when he was apologetic and needed to fix the stupid and foolish mistake he had made.

Cole knew it was wrong to invade his dad's privacy, but curiosity had gotten the best of him. He opened it and started reading.

Everything's falling apart. I used to depend on your support to help me through tough times, but I can barely keep it together anymore. God knows I haven't been a good dad to Cole either. I'm ashamed of the man I've become and I've let you down. I would give my soul just to hold you one more time...I'm lost without you.

Your loving husband,
Barrett

Cole was taken aback by the words on the card and had no idea his dad was struggling with her death, too, because he never mentioned it or talked about her. He always presented himself as the hard-edged, "I would rather take a bullet than let anyone see me cry", let's go hunt and raise some hell, tough guy. He flashed back to the shed when his dad glared at him with those bloodshot eyes. It suddenly dawned on him that they weren't bloodshot from drinking, but from crying.

"Is that why he didn't hit me?" he questioned.

He stuffed the card inside the envelope and spent several hours at his mom's grave talking to her about his problems with Mouth and Stu, his dad's drinking and reminiscing on the memorable times they had together before she got sick. It was far from the intimate conversations they used to have in the orchard, but in his heart he knew she was listening.

Monday morning didn't waste any time getting there and Cole dreaded going to school. All he could hear was Stu's voice saying "Hope you have an awesome weekend, mama's boy, because Monday's the start of a whole new week." Just the thought of Stu's obscure threat lying beneath that statement was enough to make him sick to his stomach for the rest of his life. He needed a way out of it—an excuse to stay out of school. He pretended to be sick.

His dad was in the bathroom getting ready for work. He came out and noticed Cole's bedroom door still closed.

"It's seven fifteen!" he shouted. "Time to get up!"

Cole lay in the bed, sheets pulled up to his neck, and stared at the poster of the shiny red sports car on his wall, wishing he could take off in it and leave behind the angst of Chipper Creek. His dad came back a few minutes later and pounded on the door.

"C'mon, Cole. Get the lead out."

Cole didn't budge. His dad waited for him to answer.

"Cole!" he called, and pounded again.

"I...I don't feel good," he groaned, trying to sound convincing. He waited and listened, hoping his dad would buy the sick act and leave for work.

"What's wrong with ya?"

"It's my stomach. I think I have a bug or something," he complained. "Maybe I shouldn't go to school today."

His dad turned the knob only to find it locked.

"Open the door, Cole," he demanded.

Cole could tell from the tone in his voice that he wasn't buying it.

"I really don't feel good, Dad."

"Get up and open this door!"

He procrastinated, dragging his feet as he made his way across the room. He didn't want to open it,

51

because his dad would see he was faking and punish him for lying. Then he would have to go to school anyway and take another pounding from Stu. Cole reached for the doorknob.

"It wouldn't be because of those bruises on your neck and wrists, would it?"

Cole's hand froze in mid air. His knees felt wobbly, and his guts went all knotted and queasy. This time, he really did feel sick. He was mortified, consumed by dread, because he knew that once he opened the door, it was going to be the end of him.

Dad's going to be furious, he'll yell and curse at me, and accuse me of not being a man for not standing up to them. He'll think I'm a coward, a wuss, a little bitch, just like Mouth and Stu do, and then he'll rip me a new one—an unpleasant reminder that he didn't raise me to be a "Mama's Boy".

Cole turned the knob and pulled the door back slowly with his head dropped in shame.

Scuffed toes of black leather work-boots stuck out from underneath the fraying hems of a loose-fitting set of grease-stained mechanics overalls. The white, rectangular patch over his left chest spelled out "Barrett" in dark-blue thread.

His dad stood tall and domineering with a firm expression. Cole stared blankly into his hard, unshaven face and cold blue eyes.

"I tried to fight back," he said, hoping his dad would take his efforts into consideration and go easy on him.

His dad reached out, patted him on his shoulder and said, "Get ready. I'll take you to school."

At that moment, Cole realized he wasn't about to get demolished. The two damaged souls looked at each other in silence neither one really knowing what to say, but saying more than enough and sharing the unspoken understanding.

Cole's ride to school was quiet, but comforting. His dad sipped black coffee out of an over-sized travel mug. The radio gave morning updates on the weather and traffic, and then segwayed into asking meaningless questions that enthusiastic listeners bombarded the phones to answer, all desperately needing to be the fifteenth caller to win free tickets to something.

The truck turned into the school entrance and pulled up to the student-unloading zone in front of the main building. Cole opened his door and descended onto the curb. He slung his backpack over one shoulder and looked back at his dad. His arm was relaxed and resting casually on the top of the steering wheel. He gave Cole a reassuring, but definite nod and said, "We'll take care of this. Together."

He strode up to the double-doors, undaunted, with a brighter outlook, and straighter shoulders. An irrepressible smile spread across his face, and for the first time, since before his mom died, he felt protected and safe.

Troll

Jennifer scrolled through the bombardment of new emails. Junk mostly, with promising subject lines like 15 Steps To Clear Skin, 30 Steps To A Perfect Body, 6 Ways To Get Noticed and 5 Ways To Snag A Boy; fifty-six methods instructing adolescent girls on how to become flawless or fifty-six methods on how to become flawed. What's the difference? Those deceptive tidbits of information only added to Jennifer's insecurities and frustrations by brainwashing her into believing she had to be perfect to be accepted.

As she continued searching through the assortment of electronic garbage, a suspicious email from an unknown address caught her eye. This particular email, unlike the others sitting in her inbox, wasn't random junk. It was part of a conspiracy, written with the intent to demean, belittle and destroy her. And even though it had been sent from an unknown address, Jennifer knew Kristin was the mastermind behind it. She also knew reading its content would only encourage her to internalize it, making her feel unattractive and unworthy.

They always did.

Last week's email labeled her a "Trashy Slut"; the week before that, a "Jealous Skank" and three weeks ago, she was tagged a "Dirty Whore". Jennifer didn't understand why Kristin would write such horrible things considering she had never kissed a boy, let alone slept with one. Every week a new email or text message gave her an offensive name and every week she allowed malicious rumors to gnaw at her self-confidence. Jennifer opened the message anyway, despite knowing she would hate herself afterward.

"PSYCHO BITCH!" It read in big, bold font.

Kristin had tried to soften the obvious harshness of her vile message by changing the font color from default black to bubble gum pink.

Jennifer stared blankly at the pastel obscenity and subconsciously allowed Kristin's venom to seep into the crevasses of her mind. The tasteless slur pointed its rude finger at her and she began to believe what the hateful word said.

"Am I really *psycho*?" Her words hung at the back of her throat. "Is that what everyone thinks of me?"

She stood in the full-length mirror mounted on her closet door and analyzed herself from head to toe. The lovely, mature young woman reflected back wasn't what Jennifer saw. Instead, she perceived an unattractive, even ugly, fourteen-year-old, with no poise, personality or value.

Jennifer had made the mistake of posting a "selfie" to her Facebook page. In a weak moment, she had slathered on too much make-up and posed in her sexiest outfit. Even worse, she had added a caption asking, "Do you think I'm pretty?" Ever since that posting, Kristin had been singling her out, trying to demolish her spirit and obliterate any confidence she possessed.

"What are you staring at?" Jennifer scowled at her reflection.

The image repulsed her so much she grabbed the antique, sterling silver jewelry box that had once belonged to her dearly departed grandmother, and hurled it at the mirror. Fragments of disfigured girls ogled through the web of broken glass judging and critiquing her.

"You disgust me!" Jennifer screamed, tearing herself down, and then said, "I want to look like them."

She was referring to Kristin, Leah and Jaden, the ones who had mastered the technique of ridicule and turned cyber bullying into a new art form. She wanted to look like them, even though they made fun and tormented her with vindictive pranks. Jennifer wanted to look like Kristin, Leah, and Jaden because, in her eyes, they were beautiful and appeared to have everything. There were times when she wished she knew how to sell her soul to Satan, just to have a taste of their perfect world.

Jennifer, as though she were hypnotized, walked out of the house to the slums where condemned, derelict buildings were boarded up, a perfect location to end her suffering. She was already beyond breaking point from the distressing emails, vicious text messages and other attacks. But this incident had been the most psychologically damaging.

A previous episode that played a part in her emotional breakdown was the infamous picture that spread throughout the freshman class a few months ago. The haunting photo was a candid bird's-eye-view of her, in the girls' restroom, using the toilet. Although the incriminating snapshot was taken with a cell phone, from a neighboring stall, enough evidence showed to prove it was Jennifer, like the way her hair was styled and the yellow shirt she wore that day.

By the time lunch period started, the indecent file had been uploaded, shared and viewed by most of her classmates. Boys randomly came up to her and said stuff like "Nice ass" and "Hope you wiped good."

After being freaked out by their comments, Jennifer received a text message with an attachment. There she was, hair all done up, wearing that tacky yellow shirt, buttocks jutting outward and squatting over the porcelain bowl. Totally mortified, Jennifer fled the cafeteria.

She flashed back to last week when she placed the spiral-bound notebook she used as a journal in her locker. This private rant book was an emotional outlet and a place where she could vent without getting criticized by her peers.

The college ruled pages were covered with ballpoint scribbles, self-written poems, quotes, sketches and horrible things she wished upon Kristin and her followers. There was even an earnest confession of her crush for Will Owens, the hottest boy in their class.

One day when the hall was deserted, Kristin opened Jennifer's locker to carryout one of her schemes. When the purple "truth book" fell out, she opened it and read. She laughed at Jennifer's entries, poems and feelings, then wrote PATHETIC TWAT in black marker across the cover. As she thumbed through its pages, she discovered things not intended for her eyes. Overcome with rage, Kristin had no choice but to punish Jennifer for the insults and appalling things she had written about her. Then she saw the confession. Gears turned inside her devious head and the corners of her mouth curled upward into a wicked grin. She immediately texted Jaden and Leah, notifying them about the urgent meeting she was holding after school.

When Jennifer arrived at school the following day, she found students gathered throughout the hall, phones in hand. Their eyes focused on her with disbelief and contempt.

"Way to go," one girl remarked sarcastically.

Groups of chatting busybodies disbanded and cleared a path. An uneasy feeling fell upon Jennifer as the hall grew silent. When the last huddle dispersed, she saw Will Owens standing at the end of the hall. He was reading something on his phone and wearing a disgusted look. His eyes shot up at her as she approached—those dreamy, honey eyes that stirred something deep inside her. Everyone stared, even Kristin, who stood between Leah and Jaden, arms crossed, flashing a shifty grin.

Jennifer kept a distance between herself and the heartthrob in front of her. Will finally broke the silence with a boisterous laugh.

"I don't know whether to be flattered or puke right now," he said.

Jennifer was completely clueless as to what was going on.

"What...what are you talking about?" She asked, voice trembling.

Will slowly thumbed the screen on his phone, scrolled to the top of the image that had been sent to him and a fourth of the student body, and began reading. Aloud.

"Dear Journal," he began, repressing the laughter that welled up inside him, "Will Owens is crazy hot and I think I'm in love. Every time my eyes fall upon his gorgeous face, I get all tingly. I can't tell you how many times I've imagined kissing his pouty lips. I keep having this reoccurring dream where I've had a totally crappy day at school and I'm standing at my locker, baffled by the red rose someone had placed in it. While my nose is buried deep inside the velvety folds of this long-stemmed surprise, Will sneaks up from behind, hugs me and takes me into his arms to whisk me away from the horrendous day I've had. *Sigh*."

Will's tone went all girlish and innocent-like when he said "Sigh". He was interrupted by an outburst of snickers and giggles coming from students who had lost their composure. Once the laughing stopped, he continued. "If I were pretty, he would probably ask me out. Oh, well, a girl can dream. Until next time! Jen."

An uproar of high-pitched laughter exploded from the bystanders, even though they had read it on their phones a hundred times before. Some things are just funnier when read aloud.

"Keep dreamin', psycho, because I would *never* go out with you. Friggin' gross!" Will said, and walked off.

Jennifer was speechless, disgraced and humiliated. She wanted to curl up and die. She was too stunned to blink. The awkward situation colored her face blood red, like that rose she dreamed about, and embarrassment climbed up the back of her neck. People shook their heads, pointed and laughed at her as they walked away.

Kristin, feeling proud of what she had done, sashayed up to Jennifer and said, "Now would be a good time to go kill yourself."

Jennifer, on the edge of insanity, stood on top of a three-story warehouse. Pieces of busted-out windows lay scattered across the abandoned parking lot. The glistening fragments reminded her of the mirror she smashed half an hour earlier. She tensed as her toes inched closer to the edge of the tar-patched roof, and visualized her body all mangled and twisted, down there, in a pool of blood. She wondered if her suicide would be instantaneous or would she lie in agonizing pain before succumbing to death. Everything that had driven her to this point made a premature death seem like an easy solution. Still, she wasn't sure if she could take that leap. She closed her eyes and breathed deep praying for courage, but received clarity instead.

Jennifer began to see how Kristin had manipulated her into participating in a malicious game.

An easier solution revealed itself, one that didn't involve plummeting off a warehouse roof. She realized that by reading Kristin's emails, text messages, posting pictures and comments on Facebook, she was setting herself up for ridicule and became an easy target for the Internet Trolls. Kristin and her friends had an insatiable appetite for bullying others; especially girls who they thought weren't pretty or trendy. They fed off of their victim's weaknesses to feel powerful, get more attention for themselves or impress the popular crowd.

Jennifer was wiser now. She could be more guarded with her feelings and not so quick to share her intimate thoughts on social media sites. She understood that she did not have to place herself in the middle of Kristin's web of deceit or open any of her spiteful emails ever again. By making these choices and not putting herself out there, Jennifer had the power to stop the bullying. It was that simple.

PTSD

BANG! The locker door slammed shut and Kyle freaked. He cowered in the corner beside an unsteady, mountainous heap of dirty socks infused with teenage boy sweat. He was on the floor, of this musty-smelling room where adolescent testosterone runs amuck, where offensive language is picked up and morals are dropped, where the facts of life are told in a crude joke and where weekend plans are discussed in the shower.

Kyle's knees were drawn up to his chest, arms wrapped securely around them, as if he were protecting himself from something sinister. He began rocking back and forth and stared into nothingness with a look in his eyes that could only be described as sheer terror. What was it that had him so confused and panic-stricken? And what was going on behind his huge, unblinking eyes? None of his classmates here at this new school had a clue.

I remember the horrible banging that grew louder as it approached me. It happened on a Friday evening. I know that because I had band practice after school. I was standing in the back row, near the sound proof wall and blowing hard into my tuba. I checked the clock for the time; only ten minutes left of practice, and I was glad, because it was the beginning of the weekend. Our band director sliced the air in half with her baton as we finished the last chords of the school anthem.

"Good practice everyone. We only have one week before homecoming," Mrs. Karnes reminded, "and I want everyone to give an optimal performance."

Then she dismissed us.

I opened the bulky leatherette case with the tattered, velvet interior, disassembled my instrument, and quickly shoved each section into its assigned compartment. Mrs. Karnes stopped me before I could get out the door.

"I just wanted to say, Kyle, that you have improved tremendously since the beginning of the semester and I am highly impressed with your persistence and motivation," she said.

"Thanks, Mrs. Karnes," I replied hastily, "but I *really* need to get going."

It was after five o'clock. I dashed out of the band room and raced to my locker, which was halfway across campus, in the second wing. My parents were picking me up and I didn't want to keep them waiting. But more importantly, I didn't want Scott, Cody and Travis to see me.

The second wing was death quiet and the overhead fluorescents were turned off in the hallway. The only source of light was the setting sun glaring through the wire-tempered glass in the double doors. Its warm, orange glow stretched lengthwise down the buffed hall floor.

I was busy switching out the books in my backpack when I heard that sound, that God-awful, nerve-wracking sound. BANG! My heart leaped into my throat and almost choked me. BANG! A pause, and then, BANG! Another pause. BANG! It did this over and over, each one getting closer and louder, that intimidating, gut-wrenching, BANG!

And I could feel them, those six eyes that were fixed on me—those penetrating, menacing eyes. My hands trembled as I hurriedly stuffed my books and ring binder into my bag. I reached up on the shelf for my cell phone. It was school policy to keep them in our lockers because we weren't allowed to have them in class. I crammed it in the small zippered pocket at the front of my backpack. BANG! The unsettling noise stopped at the locker beside mine and caused me to drop my belongings.

All three of them were clad in loose, basketball shorts, untied high-top sneakers and form-fitting muscle tees with the sleeves cut out. The center of their chests were soaking wet with perspiration. Layers of white sports tape were wrapped around their palms and knuckles; they had just come from hours of weight lifting in the gym, and they all stank of sweat and musky body spray.

"How's it goin', douche bag?" asked Scott.

They gathered around me. I tried to ignore them and wished with all my might that they would go away, like a bad dream, but they didn't.

"I'm taking to you, dweeb," Scott said, staring into me.

"Why don't you guys just leave me alone," I replied, trying to be nice about it. "I don't bother you."

Scott slammed his fist into the locker again. BANG! I shuddered as the noise pierced my eardrum.

"Just the sight of your geek face bothers me," he said.

"Check it out, dude," Cody observed, "he has his trombone with him."

"I bet he can blow good and hard, too," Travis snickered.

"Practice makes perfect," Cody jeered.

They were making me mad and making me late for my ride home. As I stood there, looking at those foolish meatheads who believed they were super cool and splitting their guts laughing, I thought, "What's so funny?"

"It's not a trombone, it's a tuba," I corrected, and gave Cody this "Duh" look. He wasn't the brightest one of the group.

"Keep running that mouth and I'll have to shut it up for ya," he said.

If Mrs. Karnes hadn't stopped me to commend me on my tuba playing, I could've avoided all of this. It's funny how being thrown off by a few seconds can change the course of a day.

"I gotta get going. My parents are outside waiting for me, so…"

"Awww, you gotta leave so soon?" Scott interrupted. "We thought we'd go in the restroom so you can show us how well you can blow that trombone. I bet your mouth's got mad skills."

Boisterous, despicable laughter erupted from each of them when he said that. I didn't understand why they found it funny to make me the brunt of their gay jokes. I'm not gay, and I didn't know performing in the school band made you that way. And I didn't understand why they were so determined to keep calling my tuba a trombone. In my mind I screamed, "TUBA! IT'S A TUBA! Say it with me, tooobuhhh".

They were still laughing, but by now the humor in Scott's distasteful joke had faded. They were simply laughing at me.

"It's a tuba, dumbasses!" I heard myself yell and quickly regretted saying it.

Scott laid into my chest with the side of his brawny forearm and pushed me against the locker, pinning me to it. That's when the laughter stopped.

"You're so dead," said Cody.

"You're sooo friggin' dead," Travis reiterated, stressing the amount of trouble I was in.

I know it sounds crazy, but I swear I saw flames rising in Scott's eyes as he glared hatefully into mine. Cody and Travis stood by readying themselves to take orders.

"How 'bout I shove your tuba up your queer ass?" he said, with his face just inches away from mine. The raunchy stench of cheddar cheese puffs and peanut butter rolled off his breath.

"I got a better idea," Travis proposed, "let's stuff this butt-muncher in his locker."

Then Scott smiled, really big. And before I knew what was happening, he had my shirt collar bunched up in his fist, tight enough to choke me, as he peeled me off the locker to open it.

"No! Wait! I'm sorry!" I exclaimed. "I didn't mean it! I'll never say it again. Please don't put me in there!"

I pleaded, fought, kicked and struggled, determined not to go inside that locker, because I can't handle tight spaces. Cody stepped in and helped restrain me by placing me in a headlock. The offensive odor permeating from his sweaty armpits smelled like canned chicken noodle soup. Travis tossed all my belongings off the locker shelf and onto the floor.

"Stuff his ass in there!" Scott demanded.

"No! Don't! Please!"

I started to panic when I saw they weren't kidding but actually shoving me inside, back first. I retaliated by throwing out my arms and grabbing the faces of the adjoining lockers on either side of mine, refusing to let Travis and Cody push me through the narrow opening. I was tight as a drum and wouldn't give in. The thoughts of being trapped inside that, or any confined space for that matter, freaked me out.

"Please don't put me in there!" I begged with tears swelling in my eyes.

Cody pressed down on my head making sure there was enough clearance to fit me under the shelf, Travis took hold of my ankles to tuck my legs in, and Scott stood by and watched. I clinched my teeth and put all my strength into it, resisting as much as possible, to keep them from stuffing me inside.

"Let go, you little shit!" Cody said, prying my hands off the locker frames.

My shoulders were the first inside; they brushed the cold, restricting walls of the metal box as I was forced into my phobia. Sweat seeped from every pore, my grip started to give way. Reality had set in and then I felt it, a warm stream flooding my jeans, running down my leg.

"Oh, gross!" Travis said, "The fucker's pissing himself."

It trickled over his left hand, down the sides of my shoe and onto the locker floor.

That's when Scott squeezed between the two of them, pulled his arm back and nailed my stomach with a punch I'll never forget. I slipped on my own urine and fell into the locker with an aching gut and wet jeans.

"Nighty night, freak," Scott said, slamming the door. BANG!

He made sure there was no escape by clapping the combination lock on the handle. Travis was cursing and saying something about needing to wash my pee off his hand. They laughed their way out of the building and left me there.

Inside the locker was dark and quiet. The halls screamed with an unnerving silence. My heavy breathing quickly drowned out the quiet. I was mortified. Although I had only been in the locker for a couple of minutes, I was gasping for air and felt like I was going to hyperventilate. My heart pounded in my chest. The rush of blood pulsating through my veins hummed in my ears. The crouched position I was hastily forced into was unexplainably painful. My knees trembled and rattled the walls of my prison. My shoulders were so cramped they almost met in front. Tears streamed down my face, I couldn't get a grip on my sanity or myself. I tried to kick the door; there wasn't enough room to move around. What if nobody comes down the hall? What if I have to stay locked in here until Monday morning?

"LET ME OUT!" I hollered.

I had hoped a teacher who might have stayed late or a janitor, who was sweeping a classroom at the far end of the hall, would have heard me and come down to let me out. But in the back of my mind, I knew no one was coming to save me. I was alone with my breathing, pounding heart and thoughts that betrayed me by filling my brain with horrific scenarios. There's no limit to the unimaginable things a claustrophobic person can produce in their mind when confined to tight quarters. Being trapped inside that metal coffin, I may as well have been buried alive. How insane will I get before I drift into my eternal slumber? Will I go blind first for going so long without seeing any light? Will it matter since it's dark inside the grave anyway? Will I die of fear or starvation? Is this how it feels knowing you have to spend the rest of your life with nothing but your screwed up thoughts to keep you company? Listening to your breaths grow shorter as you use up your oxygen supply and suffocate to death? How long will it take to die? Days? Weeks? Maybe months? Stop it! Stop it! I can't handle it! Where are my parents? Why haven't they come looking for me? They know I'm usually one of the first kids out the door. Don't they know something's wrong? They should suspect something by now.

If I call them to let them know I'm trapped in locker number 231, they can get me out before it's too late. Then it hit me; my phone was zipped up in the small pocket on the front of my backpack. That backpack was lying on the other side of the locker on the floor. I wondered if it were still daylight outside. Impossible. I've been in here forever. It must be nine o'clock and my parent's could care less where I am. Oh no, what if they had an accident on their way to pick me up and the police are trying to notify someone at home, but the only person who lives there, besides them, is me and I'm locked up in here!

"GET ME OUT OF HERE!" I yelled.

The locker was scorching. Sweat rolled down my back. My breathing had gotten heavier and shorter. I felt dizzy and lightheaded. I thought I was going to pass out. My legs were stiff and weak from being scrunched up for so long. Trying to shift my body to get comfortable was useless. It was too tight to move.

"Somebody, please let me out," I called in a weak, dry voice.

I needed a drink of water. After facing facts that no one was coming to my rescue and I had to spend my weekend entombed inside my locker, I closed my eyes and gave up. Then the KERCHUNK of something heavy slamming shut resounded at the opposite end of the hall. Was it the janitor locking up the double doors? I stifled my breathing and strained my ears to listen. The shuffling of shoes and the clip-clop of high heels echoed through the hallway.

"Don't worry. We'll find him," a familiar voice said.

"MRS. KARNES, HELP!" I screamed at the top of my lungs.

The shuffling footsteps raced up the hall.

"There's his backpack and tuba!"

That's mom's voice and she sounded panicked.

"I'M IN HERE!"

They rushed to my locker where my books were strewn over the floor.

"Kyle!" dad exclaimed.

"I'm in locker 231!"

"Oh good Lord!" mom screeched.

"What's your combination?" dad asked.

"Twelve right, nine left, three right, seven left and ten right," I recited. "Hurry, Dad. I can't breathe!"

The combination lock clicked as dad steadily, but hurriedly, spun the dial to each of the numbers I recited. Mom was freaking out and Mrs. Karnes did her best to calm her down. And just like that, the door opened. I fell out of my confinement, toppling onto the floor. I sucked in as much air as I could. I kicked myself as far away from that locker as possible. Its dark, gaping rectangular opening gave me the creeps. I looked up at the clock above the double-doors where the warm sunlight was still shining through.

"There's no way! It can't be! I was in there for hours!" I thought to myself, surprised to see it was only fifteen minutes til six.

Mrs. Karnes collected my books, the ones Travis had thrown out onto the floor, and neatly stacked them on the locker shelf. Totally oblivious to the trauma I was suffering, she slammed the door. BANG! I threw my hands over my ears to block out that atrocious noise.

Kyle was still in the locker room sitting next to the dirty sock pile. He had rocked back and forth for several minutes. Sharp elbows pointed outward as he covered his ears to block out the maddening sound of the slamming locker door. His eyes were shut tight and his teeth were clinched. Once the fear had dissipated from his face, he opened his eyes and blinked twice. He was slowly coming around.

Being shoved into that locker had left a scar on Kyle's emotional psyche. It was because of that incident that his parents found it necessary to transfer him here, to this school, but that wasn't the solution. The repercussions from his ordeal will always remain no matter where he goes.

Superhero

Taylor wished Luke and A.J. dead. He wanted the unspeakable to happen to them.

"They shouldn't have done it," he said. "They shouldn't have ganged up on me and called me that."

"That" meaning, "Cocksucking Retard".

Once, after having a brief skirmish with A.J. during second period lunch, Taylor cursed him with a beginner's Wiccan spell he found online and a couple of days later, A.J. fell sick with the flu. Taylor wasn't completely sure if the illness was mere coincidence, but he flattered himself by believing he was the cause of it. His overactive imagination had always been an outlet for his repressed emotions. Sometimes, when things got really bad, he entertained the idea of possessing superpowers, which would come in handy after being verbally bashed and attacked at school. It plays out with him finding a secluded, dark corner somewhere, transforming into a masked, chisel-chested giant and then reappearing at the most opportune time to teach Luke and A.J. a lesson.

But that was just a fantasy.

In real-life, he sat in his bedroom with the door locked, music blaring and pressed the steel blade of his mom's paring knife into his flesh. He pulled back, slowly, diagonally, dragging it across the tender side of his arm, just below the bend of his elbow and watched the crimson liquid rise to the surface. Swelled droplets traced the rut of his protruding veins as it traveled downward to his wrist and dripped onto the leg of his jeans. He closed his sorrowful eyes and allowed the pressures from his day at school to trickle out of him. Like his colorful imagination this, too, was a ritual he performed to escape his frustrations when he's had more than he could tolerate.

Cutting his arm didn't really make Taylor feel better; it was simply the point of being able to feel something more painful than what he was feeling emotionally that helped him cope. Both limbs had been hacked on so many times he was running out of places to cut and, eventually, he would have to start on his legs. Taylor concealed his shame by wearing long sleeves, even during the summer. This resulted in more rude stares and vulgar comments from his peers at school, because it seemed to confirm their accusations about him being a weirdo, a freak, a total moron.

The release was soothing and calming as Luke and A.J.'s abuse bled out of him like a toxic sickness. After spending fifteen minutes easing his pain, Taylor cleaned up the blood with a dark shirt, took off his jeans, sprayed them down with stain remover and immediately tossed them in the washing machine. He threw on a pair of sweatpants, a long-sleeved tee and sat down in front of the computer to log onto his social media account. One person had commented on the picture he posted of his pet Chihuahua.

"That pint-sized mutt is for wusses," it read. "Get a real dog, loser!"

The profile picture to the left of the comment was a cropped shot of a torso with the shirt raised halfway to reveal a set of abs. Luke thought himself a ripped Spartan warrior and loved showing those bumps off at any given chance. Like during PE for example, he always removed his shirt just to make two warm-up laps around the gym.

A.J. had approved Luke's comment by checking "I Like This" and on some miniscule level the nasty remark had struck a chord with Taylor. His unsteady, twitching fingers hovered over the keyboard as he searched the ceiling for the appropriate words to respond with. He knew firing back some irreverent statement would only get him into serious trouble later, so he backed-off and deleted Luke's profane comment.

Taylor's mom had come home from work and was in the kitchen preparing dinner before the man-of-the-house got home. Taylor could hear her futzing around in there rattling pots and pans under the cabinets as she took one, two, three of them out and placed them on the counter. Next, she opened one, two, three cabinet drawers, then four, five, six of them, just opening and closing, opening and closing, as she searched. Taylor was still glued in front of his computer looking at mindless teenager stuff when she peeked her head in.

"Taylor, honey, have you seen my paring knife?" She asked, all motherly and sweet-like.

His back faced the bedroom door. She couldn't see the "Holy Crap!" expression that painted his face when she asked that. Taylor shamefully dropped his left hand into his lap, under the computer desk, and inconspicuously worked the cuff of the long-sleeved T-shirt over the heel of his palm. He clutched it with his fingers, to hold it in place, like the sleeve was going to magically roll up on it's own and reveal what he had been doing in his bedroom with her paring knife—the same paring knife that he confiscated months ago and hid under the head of his mattress. He guiltily clutched that shirt cuff, holding it tight, as if he had been caught or like she had peeked her head in and demanded, "TAYLOR! SHOW ME YOUR ARM!"

He sat there for a moment, pretending to be enthralled with the page on his screen and replied, "Huh? Knife? No...I haven't seen it."

Mrs. Bradshaw was out that day and fifth period English was being conducted by a substitute. Taylor knew he was in for it with Luke and A.J., because being afraid of a substitute teacher was like being afraid of a rent-a-cop at the mall. No one respected them and this rent-a-teacher wouldn't be able to keep Luke and A.J. in line.

"Settle down, settle down," the substitute said, her passive voice barely above a whisper.

Yep. Taylor was in for it.

"My name is Ms. Hall and I'm your substitute for the day. Mrs. Bradshaw left very specific instructions for you to continue working on your research papers on a well-known American author."

Luke was sprawled and laid back in his seat. Mister Badass. He shot up his index finger to ask a question.

"Yes?" she asked.

"Yeah, uh," Luke began, voice all deep, "can we leave if we're done?" he asked, testing the waters.

A.J. and the rest of the class chuckled. Ms. Hall looked about the room at the faces giggling at her expense.

"Why? Have you finished with yours?" she asked.

"No. I haven't even started mine."

The class laughed again.

"Well, I'm afraid not," she replied.

Taylor's guts felt queasy and bubbled like he had eaten some rotten fish sticks. He kept his head down, afraid to look up. It was going to be the longest hour of his life.

As soon as Ms. Hall turned her back to write on the board, A.J., being all stealthy, left his seat and slipped into the empty one behind Luke. Taylor set his controls to high alert mode, because he knew they were plotting something. Something huge.

The first half of class went by with no problems until all of a sudden, thump! A pencil had been launched across the room at rapid speed and bounced off the side of Taylor's head. It hit the floor and rolled under the bookcase where Mrs. Bradshaw kept extra copies of textbooks, thesauruses, packs of copy paper and other teaching materials. Luke and A.J. snickered four rows away. Taylor continued writing his works cited page and ignored them, although he was getting warm under his collar.

Then, a few minutes later, FLOP! Taylor's left cheek stung and throbbed after a hefty, paperback book that came out of nowhere walloped him and landed face-up on his desk. A thick, well-used copy of Merriam Webster's stared him in the face. Taylor, with his head angled sideways, shot his eyes over at them. The two pals were laughing quietly amongst themselves as they watched from afar, getting kicks out of teasing him and knowing the rent-a-teacher wasn't going to do anything about it. Luke stopped laughing and began moving his lips. Nothing came out, but Taylor clearly read them as Luke called him a "Pussy."

Taylor submerged himself in his rage, embarrassment and isolation—the way he always felt after being attacked. He needed his mom's paring knife, desperately, like a cocaine addict needed a quick fix. He needed to push up his sleeve and filet his arm to ease the pressure. He needed to get a grip on his emotions before he freaked out in front of the entire class.

How would that look?

The overactive imagination took over, and using his special powers to transform, Taylor reenters Mrs. Bradshaw's American English class irrefutably confident, beefy, masked and unannounced, to confront the villains in the back row.

"You want to throw dictionaries and sharp pencils at people? Then throw them at me!" he thunders with solid arms folded across a broad, heaving chest. "I dare you!"

Luke and A.J. run off at the mouth, the signature defense of all cowards. They find things from around the classroom to hurl: books, pencils, ink pens, curse words, a stapler, notebooks, wads of paper, more curse words. The avenger they don't recognize stands firm, unwavering and courageous as the objects and obscenities bounce off of him.

"It takes more than a few books and vile words to hurt me!" he explodes, and takes a giant leap towards them.

A.J. and Luke stand their ground, fists up and ready to fight. The superhero cracks his knuckles, makes a super-sized fist and sucker punches Luke, almost breaking his jaw. POW! He tumbles to the floor, and then A.J. steps up to try his luck, only to have his breath knocked out of him by the black boot that gets planted in his abdomen. WHAM! He ascends through the air and slams into Mrs. Bradshaw's bookcase where the torpedo pencil that started it all is still hiding underneath. CRASH! Already accepting their defeat, they shield their faces and beg for mercy.

"Okay, okay! We give up," Luke says in a trembling voice. "You win!"

"We just wanted to have some fun. We didn't mean to hurt anybody," A.J. whines, holding his gut.

"You think calling people names, throwing things at them and bullying them is fun? I should use my special powers to eliminate the both of you!"

"No! Please don't!" Luke shouts. "We've learned our lesson. We won't pick on anyone else. We swear!"

Fearless, squinted eyes penetrate the evil duo through the eyeholes of his high-tech mask.

"Hmmm, I guess I could give you another chance to mend your ways. But I'll be watching you. And no more bully business. Got it?" he says in a stern voice.

Luke and A.J. quickly nod their heads as a promise to stop their ruthless shenanigans.

"Or else," he warns, and sprints out of the room.

The loud buzz of the school bell snapped Taylor back to reality. He procrastinated so he could be the last one out of the classroom and to put distance between himself, A.J. and Luke.

Taylor slammed the bedroom door and tossed his books onto the unmade flannel sheets, just before falling into the swivel chair at his computer. He

94

anxiously bobbed his right leg up and down, and lost himself within the screensaver of the animated ball bouncing across the monitor. He wiggled the mouse to wake the computer out of hibernation mode and logged into his social media account. A shared link titled, "LMAO! U GOTTA C THIS! 2 FUNNY!" waited in his messages. Unsure of who sent it, but curious to know what the file was, Taylor clicked on it.

His expression morphed from the confused look of uncertainty to wide-eyed horror within a matter of seconds. He couldn't believe what he was seeing. There, on his computer screen, was a cell phone recorded video of the airborne dictionary crashing into the side of his face. It began with him sitting at his desk, working on his research paper and all of a sudden a fat paperback book comes hurling across the room, pages flapping, and then FLOP! The humiliating clip pushed him closer to the edge as he watched in horror. The embarrassment and rage he felt when it happened was intense, but nothing came close to the feeling that boiled within him from watching Luke and A.J.'s malicious prank a disgusting, repulsive feeling that resembled hate, but felt a hundred times worse. He was beside himself with anger and completely mortified as the three-second crash replayed over and over. He wondered how many kids at school had already seen the degrading footage and laughed themselves sick over it. How many had added sound effects with their mouths? How many had texted each other about Luke and A.J.'s homemade video gone viral? Taylor couldn't handle it. He locked the door and reached under the mattress for his mom's misplaced paring knife.

Lunch period is the most important period of any school day. It gives teens something to look forward to while they're sitting through grueling classes. For Taylor, eating lunch in the cafeteria was not an option and he stayed well clear of it. He didn't like being in that unsupervised, free-for-all setting, surrounded by people who didn't understand him. He didn't like being in there, because it made him edgy and paranoid, and was the best place to get picked on. Taylor didn't like eating lunch in the cafeteria, because Luke and A.J. were in there.

Instead, he sat at the far end of the hall, resting against the lockers, knees drawn and eating the bag lunch he brought from home. He preferred it this way, he didn't have to endure the unpleasantness of being singled-out or shunned when he sat down at a table or being attacked by french fries, chicken strips, pizza bites and other food items that could be launched in his direction. Taylor's private lunchtime, in the hall, was the only place he could chill-out and be himself.

He stared at the bottom of the lockers across from him and drifted to the episode in American English class. The humiliation he suffered, after being assaulted by the dictionary, weighed on his shoulders. Reflecting on Luke and A.J. snickering across the room, and the recorded event posted online, started to pick at the wound that was still fresh and raw. Two pair of legs in distressed jeans blocked Taylor's view and interrupted his daydream. He looked up to find Luke and A.J. smirking at him.

"What?" Taylor asked defensively.

"You're a freakin' retard, that's what," A.J. replied, "and everybody knows it."

"Why don't you eat in the cafeteria like normal people?" Luke asked.

Taylor ignored them and washed his food down with the last swallow of fruit punch.

Luke kicked the side of Taylor's shoe.

"Hey, jerk-off, are you deaf? I'm talkin' to you!" he shouted, drawing attention from the few students who were standing close by.

Taylor pretended he didn't hear him. He snatched the brown paper bag, grabbed his books and walked the opposite direction to remove himself from the problem.

"Hey, bro!" Luke called out. "How'd you like that link I sent you? Pretty cool, huh?"

Taylor stopped walking. His face turned various shades of red and that strange, repulsive feeling he felt in his bedroom started churning in his stomach.

"Dude, it's even funnier if you watch it in slow mo." A.J. said, trying to provoke him. "He looks like he's about to shit himself when that dictionary smacks him in the face."

Taylor shut his eyes and counted to ten and took a few deep breaths to brush off their comments, but he couldn't.

Enough was enough.

He turned around and pushed his sleeves up past his elbows. Gasps were heard from the bunch lining the hall as he revealed the scars from the paring knife, including the fresh one that was scabbed over. The simple gesture put to rest everyone's suspicions of why he wore those long-sleeved shirts and crushed their accusations of him being a freak, weirdo and a total moron. Now they could see him for who he really was, a damaged kid trying to deal with the pressures of high school and trying find his own way.

He bravely sauntered up to Luke and A.J. who were standing in the middle of the hall wearing crooked smiles and feeling noble. Taylor stood eye to eye to them. He didn't cringe, tremble, or blink.

"First off, I'm not your 'bro' and second, it must really suck to have nothing better to do than just sit around and find ways to mess with people."

"Excuse me?" Luke asked, taken aback by Taylor's audacity.

"You heard. I'm not putting up with you or anymore of your bullshit!" Taylor took another step closer. "It stops right now!"

"Dude, are you really being serious right now?" A.J. chuckled.

Taylor threw A.J. a look that could have burned his eyeballs out of their sockets and said, "I'm dead serious. I'm not letting either of you bully me anymore!"

"Whatever. Bro," A.J. huffed, shrugging off Taylor's demand.

"Why don't you get out of my face before everyone sees me kick your ass?" Luke suggested.

Taylor scowled through squinted eyes. "Why don't you go screw yourselves? You're always up each other's ass anyway."

A couple of students giggled at the bold comeback. Luke and A.J. felt their egos being stripped away as Taylor cut them down a notch.

"I'm gonna stomp your ass up and down this hall," declared Luke, and shoved Taylor in his chest with both hands.

He stumbled backward and fell. The few students who were gathered around started getting restless and excited, awaiting the next move. Taylor jumped to his feet and planted them on the floor.

His nostrils flared and the overflow of adrenaline pumping through his veins caused him to tremble. He fixed his eyes on his opponent, drew his fingers into a tight fist and put all he had into it. But the punch barely made it. It whizzed through the air and caught Luke in the lower jaw, between his cheek and mouth.

A roar from the bystanders resonated throughout the hall as the first punch had been thrown. Taylor brought up his other arm to launch another one, but Luke caught it in mid air and drilled his fist in Taylor's stomach. It was the first time he had ever been socked in the gut and it hurt something fierce. He fell back against a locker, sucking up the pain.

"You should learn to keep that big trap of yours shut," Luke said, and commenced to pound Taylor's face.

He would have preferred the sting of the dictionary any day to the throbbing pain that ran through his jaws, teeth and skull.

"How does it feel to be the piece-of-shit who's getting his ass kicked?" asked Luke.

Taylor glanced up at him and said, "The same as it does to be the asshole that's too much of a wimp to fight someone his own size."

Luke's eyes bulged with fury and Taylor braced himself for what happened next. The extra helping of knuckle sandwiches caused him to see double and hear bells. Luke wasn't letting up and the punches kept coming. Taylor needed a way out of his predicament. He was backed against the locker, shielding his face from the impact of boulder fists laying into it and couldn't get loose. His only alternative was to bring up his knee and ram it into Luke's groin.

A gust of air, followed by a mammoth curse word, escaped Luke's mouth as he doubled over from the sharp flash of pain in his crotch. It tore through his perfect abs and felt like his chest was caving in.

Taylor pried himself off the locker, shook the ringing out of his head and put up his fists preparing to swing. He caught a glimpse of A.J.'s fist coming at him through his peripheral vision. He ducked, missing the strike by a hair, but he was still at a disadvantage. He couldn't fend off both of them. None of the students who watched the unfair fight jumped in to help even the odds. Luke had recovered and came back swinging. Taylor danced and darted to keep from getting pounded, but one brain rattling punch from A.J. knocked his head sideways and everything went white. He lay numb and powerless on the floor. Thunderous shouts and cheers rang out from the crowd surrounding him.

"Get up!" A.J. demanded.

Taylor didn't budge.

"What's the matter? You had enough?"

Although he was whipped and knew he couldn't possibly win the fight, Taylor flashed a large grin.

"What the hell are you smiling at?" A.J. asked.

"Yeah, cumbag, what's so funny?" Luke questioned. "You want some more?"

Luke and A.J. couldn't comprehend how Taylor could be grinning after the battle he had just lost, not to mention the humiliation and embarrassment he brought upon himself for even trying.

But winning the fight wasn't his objective. Acknowledging his self-worth and owning the courage to stand up to his tormentors is what gave him ultimate gratification. Taylor lay on the floor smiling, because within himself, he found a Superhero.

About The Author

James Penn is a native of Mount Airy, North Carolina. He is a graphic designer, illustrator and instructor. His knowledge in the field is shared among his students at Surry Community College where he teaches in the Advertising and Graphic Design department.

Possessing a creative talent and having an interest in social issues, the inspiration for Affliction transpired when staggering reports of bullying first began making headlines. Bullying is a problem for many kids and teens, and shouldn't be ignored or taken lightly. Hopefully, this book will encourage all members of society to make a difference and help eradicate the unwarranted mistreatment of today's youth.

James would like to hear from his readers. You can contact him via email: afflictionbook@yahoo.com

About The Illustrations

When I began making plans for the layout of Affliction, two major elements needed to be in place: intriguing, lifelike stories and captivating illustrations.

As a graphic design instructor, I consider myself privileged to teach a wide range of students who are exceptionally talented and possess unique, individual styles—I had to have that combination in my book. Narrowing my selection to Tyler Stachowicz and Jeff Skidmore was based solely on their artistic vision, creative flair and ability to place themselves in the character's situation, and then convey that feeling in a black and white illustration. Giving the illustrators free reign, allowing them to execute their ideas in their medium of choice, added another layer of depth and realism to the book.

Using various techniques from pen and ink, marker, ink wash and Adobe Photoshop, these young artists effectively captured the mood of each story.

A Special Thanks

To my close friends and family who offered constructive criticism and gave me their full support during the conception of this book, Gloria Lawrence, my elementary school reading teacher and editor, who provided the finishing touches to this project with her grammatical expertise, Lowanda Badgett, my high school creative writing teacher, whose class awakened the tiny author inside, and to my brilliant illustrators, Tyler Stachowicz and Jeff Skidmore—phenomenal work, guys!

www.ingramcontent.com/pod-product-compliance
Lightning Source LLC
Chambersburg PA
CBHW070636130626
46555CB00006B/2568